place a photo of you and your Nana here

Also by Irene Smalls:

BECAUSE YOU'RE LUCKY ❧ JONATHAN AND HIS MOMMY
IRENE AND THE BIG, FINE NICKEL ❧ KEVIN AND HIS DAD

To my Nana, who taught me "I love you Black Child" —I.S.

Clarence Pierce

Louise Godfrey McNeil, Irene's Nana

For our very special Nana Lucille — thanks, Mom —C.A.J.

Little, Brown and Company

Time Warner Book Group
1271 Avenue of the Americas, New York, NY 10020
Visit our Web site at www.lb-kids.com

First Edition

10 9 8 7 6 5 4 3 2 1

SC

Manufactured in China

The text for this book was set in Hoffman, and the display type is Ruzicka
Freehand and Wendy.

The illustrations were done in water-based paints on Crescent Strathmore
watercolor board.

Book design by Tracy Shaw

Library of Congress Cataloging-in-Publication Data

Smalls-Hector, Irene.
My Nana and me / by Irene Smalls ; illustrated by Cathy Ann Johnson—1st ed.
     p. cm.
Summary: A young girl and her grandmother enjoy a day filled with tea parties,
     hide-and-seek, stories, and plenty of love.
ISBN 0-316-16821-1
[1. Grandmothers—Fiction. 2. Play—Fiction. 3. African Americans—Fiction.] I.
     Johnson, Cathy Ann, 1964- ill. II. Title.

PZ7.S63915My 2004
[E]—dc22

2003056318

My Nana and Me

by Irene Smalls   Illustrated by Cathy Ann Johnson

LITTLE, BROWN AND COMPANY

New York ∾ Boston

My Nana and me had a tea party
and all my dolls came
We had tea and cake and ate and ate

bread puddin' and apple pie

I wore Nana's Sunday hat and shoes
I put on a show
I danced like a ballerina and sang
My Nana

clapped and clapped and clapped

Then we played hide-and-seek
My Nana can never find me
I am the smartest girl in the world
I know because my Nana told me so

and she knows everything

My Nana's a giant — she's so tall
She can reach and touch the sky
She has a big, long skirt
that I hide behind sometimes

Then Nana calls me her baby girl, but I'm

not a baby, I'm big

My Nana gets down on her knees to talk to me
We rub noses

the way Eskimos kiss

I comb and plait my Nana's hair

Overbraid and underbraid,

Overbraid and underbraid.

Next we play pat-a-cake till half past eight

That's when I take a bath
My Nana washes me with hands that tickle my nose and dance on my back
as she sings,

"Onchi monchi bunchi bunch,
onchi monchi bunchi bunch"

She calls me her sweetening girl
and laughs and laughs and laughs
She sits me on her knee and reads to me
story after story after story

When I ask Nana why am I her sweetening girl
Nana says because there's a sky
because there's a sea
but mostly

because there is me

Then, Nana
such a sleepyhead
lies down on my bed
and then

so do I